Chinese History Stories ❧

Stories from the Imperial Era
221BC-AD1912

Translated from the original Chinese by Qian Jifang
❧ Edited by Renee Ting

✤ A Brief Introduction to Chinese History

The history of China dates back thousands of years, but it wasn't always the big, unified country we know today. In early Chinese history, about 4,000 years ago, China was a much smaller area of land, governed by kings. As the kings passed their power down to their sons, the first dynasties began. There were no written records until the third dynasty, the Zhou dynasty.

The Zhou dynasty was the longest dynasty in Chinese history, lasting from 1122-221 BC. At that time, kings did not yet call themselves emperors and the truth was, they did not have much control over areas far from their own capital. Instead, they granted land to their relatives, friends, and valued followers, who controlled each area themselves. At first, the capital of the Zhou dynasty was located in the western area of the land, but after a rebellion in 771 BC, the new king moved it to the east. Historians thus divide the Zhou dynasty into two periods: the Western Zhou and the Eastern Zhou.

After the capital was moved to the east, local rulers took control over their land and people, creating many small states. Each state was ruled by its own government. Moreover, the states began fighting each other for power and land. This period of fighting during the Eastern Zhou dynasty was called the Spring and Autumn period (771-481 BC), named after a famous book written by the great Chinese philosopher Confucius.

At first, the leaders of the fighting states called themselves dukes, but as they grew stronger, they grew bolder and began to consider themselves kings. The strongest kings defeated the weaker states, and when there were only seven strong states left, the Warring States period (403-221 BC) began. Each of the seven states was independently ruled by its own king, and all of them were constantly occupied by fighting or forming alliances with each other.

In 221 BC, the king of the Qin state conquered all the other states and unified the country of China. He gave himself the name Qin Shi Huangdi, meaning "First Emperor of Qin," and claimed that his power was bestowed upon him by Heaven. He also named his unified country Zhong Guo, meaning "Middle Kingdom," and considered it the center of the universe, while all people outside it were thought to be barbarians.

Normally, each emperor would name one of his sons the Crown Prince, who would then become the next emperor. As long as the power stayed within the family, the dynasty would continue. However, the government in power had to always be alert for rebellions. Sometimes, after a period of fighting, the rebels would win power over the country, and a new dynasty would begin.

Over the next 2,000 years, China was ruled by this system of imperial monarchy. From the Qin dynasty to the last dynasty of Qing, there were fourteen different dynasties, though some were ruled by foreign invaders. Of all the dynasties, a few stand out for their contributions to the culture and history of China. The Qin dynasty is known for the building of the Great Wall, and for the terracotta soldiers in the First Emperor's tomb. The Han dynasty was a time of great strength and extended the Chinese territory westward. The Tang dynasty was a time of flourishing art and poetry. The final dynasty, the Qing, was one of the strongest and most prosperous, encompassing the largest area of land in China's history, until it was weakened by oppression from western countries. In 1912, the Qing dynasty was overthrown by a democratic movement led by Sun Yat Sen and the Republic of China was established. In 1949, the Communist Party, headed by Mao Zedong, took control and renamed the country the People's Republic of China. It is still governed by the Communist Party today.

The eight stories selected for this volume of Chinese History Stories come from the 2,000-year period of imperial rule, from 221 BC until AD 1912. They introduce some of the most famous and beloved figures from this period, including military heroes, clever officials, and even a princess. The stories take place in wartime and in peaceful times, and reflect the spirit of a mighty nation struggling to grow with the changing world around it.

These stories have been passed down for so many generations that the characters and the places they made famous have become legendary. If you visit China today, you can still see many of the landmarks, monuments, and temples built at the time these stories took place, over 2,000 years ago. Join us on a journey into the past of ancient China, and meet the people who shaped its history and live on in the hearts of Chinese people today.

✤ Timeline of Chinese History

XIA DYNASTY	2205-1776 BC
SHANG DYNASTY	1766-1122 BC
ZHOU DYNASTY	1122-221 BC
Western Zhou	1122-771 BC
Eastern Zhou	771-221 BC
Spring and Autumn	771-481 BC
Warring States	403-221 BC
QIN DYNASTY	221-207 BC
HAN DYNASTY	207 BC - AD 220
THREE KINGDOMS/PERIOD OF DIVISION	220-589
SUI DYNASTY	589-618
TANG DYNASTY	618-907
FIVE DYNASTIES AND TEN KINGDOMS PERIOD	907-960
SONG DYNASTY	960-1279
YUAN DYNASTY	1279-1368
MING DYNASTY	1368-1644
QING DYNASTY	1644-1912
REPUBLIC OF CHINA	1912-1949
PEOPLE'S REPUBLIC OF CHINA	1949-present

✤ Reading Chinese

In 1958, a spelling system called pinyin was developed so that the Roman alphabet could be used to spell out Chinese characters. The system could represent both the sound and the tone of each character using letters and a selection of accent marks. In this book, we have used the pinyin system without the accent marks for the sake of simplicity. Also, some letters are pronounced differently in pinyin than they are in English. Here are a few examples:

zh = j Example: Zhou = joh
q = ch Example: Qin = cheen
x = sh Example: Xun Xi = shoon shee

❖ Contents

✦The Banquet at Hongmen

鸿门宴

After the death of the first Emperor of the Qin dynasty (221-207 BC), the second Emperor of Qin ascended to the throne. He was even more merciless and brutal than the first and people throughout China despised and feared him. There was widespread unrest and rebellious forces began to gain strength. Xiang Liang, a man from Chu, led the strongest force. Among his troops, two important figures emerged: his nephew Xiang Yu and a southern farmer named Liu Bang.

Through the years, Xiang Liang recruited a large number of followers and he built a strong army. One day, a resourceful man named Fan Zeng came to see him. He proposed a plan for Xiang Liang to gain great power without risking his position.

"Even though we are ruled by the Qin emperor," he told Xiang Liang, "the common people still cherish their homeland of Chu. If you can establish a member of the Chu royal family as king, the men who were loyal to Chu will come back and fight for you."

Xiang Liang found a grandson of the former king and set him up as King Huai of Chu. To try to speed up the collapse of Qin, King Huai of Chu issued a decree: "Whoever can conquer the capital of Qin will be recognized by all as the King of Guanzhong."

The Guanzhong region around Qin's capital was the richest and most influential area of China. To rule Guanzhong was to rule all of China.

The king sent Xiang Liang to the north to fight Qin's main forces. During a fierce battle, Xiang Liang was killed. His nephew, Xiang Yu, took his place as the rebel leader. Xiang Yu, raised by his uncle, was ambitious. He wanted to become the Emperor of Qin someday. He avenged his uncle's death by repeatedly defeating Qin's main forces in the north.

Meanwhile, a young man named Liu Bang, who was raised on a farm in the south of China, led a group from his home state to join the rebellion. He battled his way successfully westward toward Guanzhong.

By the time Xiang Yu fought his way to the Hangu Pass, also known as the Gate to Guanzhong, he found Liu Bang's troops already defending the pass. Though they both fought on the side of the rebellion, Xiang Yu wanted to be the one to take the capital of Qin. When he heard a rumor that Liu Bang had already taken the capital, Xiang Yu and his troops broke through the defenses at the Hangu Pass. Once inside Guanzhong, he and his 400,000 men made camp at Hongmen, a city not far from the capital.

In reality, Liu Bang and his 10,000 men had not yet occupied the capital and were stationed at another city called Ba, only a few dozen miles from Hongmen.

One of Liu Bang's highest officers sent a soldier to Xiang Yu with a secret message. "Beware: Liu Bang intends to occupy the capital and become King of Guanzhong, keeping all its treasures for himself."

Xiang Yu angrily ordered his troops to prepare for an attack on Liu Bang's camp. His advisor Fan Zeng urged him to act quickly to put an end to this threat.

One of Xiang Yu's men named Xiang Bo heard this plan. He had a friend who was the top counselor to Liu Bang and worried for his friend's life. Xiang Bo took a horse and galloped immediately to Liu Bang's camp. When he found his friend, Zhang Liang, he urged him to escape before the attack, which was sure to be deadly. However, Zhang Liang would not desert Liu Bang. Instead of fleeing, he reported the news to his commander.

Alarmed, Liu Bang asked Zhang Liang for his advice. "My Lord, do you think that our troops are a match for Xiang Yu's troops?" Zhang Liang asked.

After some thought, Liu Bang replied, "No, we would not be able to withstand an attack. What should we do?" Zhang Liang proposed having his friend Xiang Bo take a message back to Xiang Yu.

Liu Bang agreed
and said to Xiang Bo, "Please tell Xiang Yu that although my troops
entered Guanzhong first, I dared not touch a thing. I made a register of the
citizens, sealed the storehouses, and camped out here to await the arrival of
Commander Xiang. I only sent men to guard the Hangu Pass to keep
out bandits. We hoped Commander Xiang would arrive quickly. Why would
we rebel against him? Please convey to him my sincerity."

Xiang Bo agreed to give the message to Xiang Yu, but added, "You must
come early tomorrow morning and apologize in person."

Liu Bang promised.

When Xiang Bo returned to his camp, he went straight to Xiang Yu to relay the message. "Liu Bang took Guanzhong first only to clear the way so that you could enter easily. If we attack him, we would be acting dishonorably. We should treat him respectfully when he arrives."
Xiang Yu nodded in agreement.

The next morning, Liu Bang and a hundred of his men arrived at Hongmen. He bowed to Xiang Yu with respect and said, "Please believe me, I was not expecting to be the first to enter Guanzhong. Someone sowed doubt in your mind so that you would distrust me."

"It was your own general who sent the information," replied Xiang Yu. "Now that the misunderstanding has been cleared up, please join us for a banquet tonight as our honored guest."

That evening, both sides dined together. Throughout the meal, the advisor, Fan Zeng, tried to hint to his commander, Xiang Yu, to take the opportunity to kill Liu Bang. Fan Zeng grew frustrated when Xiang Yu did nothing. Taking matters into his own hands, Fan Zeng excused himself and went to find a guard in Xiang Yu's inner circle.

"Our lord is too kindhearted to have Liu Bang killed," he said. "You must do the job. Go in and drink a toast, then offer to perform a sword dance. Seize that chance to kill Liu Bang. He is too dangerous. If he lives, we will all end up as his subjects some day and that would be intolerable."

The swordsman did as he was told and entered the banquet hall.

"Our Lord and Lord Liu Bang are feasting and drinking, but there is no entertainment," he said. "May I perform a sword dance for you?"

"Very well," said Xiang Yu.

Once the assassin drew his sword, Xiang Bo did the same. Throughout the dance, Xiang Bo maneuvered himself in between the assassin and Liu Bang at all times, preventing the swordsman from attacking.

Seeing this, Liu Bang's adviser and friend of Xiang Bo's, Zhang Liang slipped outside to find a general who was keeping watch outside the banquet.

The general asked Zhang Liang, "How goes it inside?"

"Badly," Zhang Liang replied. "There is a man performing a sword dance. Clearly, they intend to kill our lord."

"This is serious!" The general was enraged. "I'm going in!"

Xiang Yu's guards tried to block him from entering,
but the general knocked them down easily with his shield.

The general was incensed and stood by his lord,
Liu Bang. His piercing glare was a clear message of his anger.

Xiang Yu casually rested his hand on his sword hilt,
took a drink, and raised himself up on one knee.
"And who might this newcomer be?" he asked.

"He is one of Lord Liu Bang's generals, Fan Kuai,"
Zhang Liang answered.

"Welcome, then!" said Xiang Yu. "Give this stout fellow a goblet of wine and a leg of pork."

General Fan Kuai drank the wine in one gulp and set his shield on the ground. He placed the pork on his shield and using his sword, cut off a chunk of meat and began to eat.

"I'm not afraid of death," he said to Xiang Yu. "So, I will speak my mind.

"The Emperor of Qin was a cruel and heartless man, torturing and killing so many people that the rest of the world rose up to revolt against him. Here, Lord Liu Bang has entered Guanzhong, but took nothing, withdrawing his troops and waiting for your arrival. Though he has served you loyally, he is greeted with punishment instead of praise simply because you believed lies from a traitor's mouth. You are treading the same path toward your downfall as the Emperor of Qin. I beg you to rethink your actions, My Lord."

Xiang Yu was speechless. After a while, Liu Bang excused himself and beckoned General Fan Kuai to accompany him.

Once outside, Liu Bang said, "My life is surely still in danger. I should use this opportunity to escape, but it would be rude to leave without a word."

"Too much care of minor details spoil big plans," replied Fan Kuai. "In there, we are like meat on the kitchen block, ready for chopping. This is no time for politeness."

Zhang Liang joined them then to see what the delay was. Liu Bang asked him to wait until he had been gone long enough to reach his own camp, then return to the banquet to make his apologies and present gifts.

When enough time had passed, Zhang Liang returned to the banquet and told Xiang Yu, "Lord Liu Bang has departed. He had drunk a bit too much and was unable to make his farewells himself. He asked me to present this pair of white jade disks to Your Lordship and this pair of jade wine cups to Fan Zeng."

"Where is Lord Liu Bang now?" asked Xiang Yu.

"He was worried about your accusation, so he departed Hongmen and should be back at our camp by now."

Xiang Yu gracefully accepted the jade disks, but Fan Zeng threw the jade cups to the ground, drew his sword, and smashed them to pieces.

"These men will not amount to anything," he said. "They won't take my advice. Lord Xiang Yu will lose this empire to Lord Liu Bang. We will all end up as Liu Bang's subjects one day!"

As for Liu Bang, as soon as he returned to his camp, he executed the man who told the rumors to Xiang Yu. Years later, Fan Zeng's prediction came true. Liu Bang defeated Xiang Yu and became the first Emperor of the Han dynasty.

Illustrations by Hu Zhiming

Learn more

After the death of the first Qin emperor, his second son, Hu Hai succeeded as the second Qin emperor. Hu Hai's father had written a letter to the eldest son to make him the next emperor, but Hu Hai, with the help of the prime minister, destroyed the letter. He also had anyone who opposed him as emperor killed, including his siblings. He was a weak leader, only interested in a life of luxury. The Qin dynasty ended after a peasant rebellion, lasting only 15 years and two generations.

With the end of the Qin dynasty began the Han dynasty, which lasted for 426 years. The rulers of this dynasty tried to soften some of the harsher aspects of the Qin dynasty. They decreased taxes and appointed people to the government based on merit rather than family ties. They followed the teachings of Confucius. They also expanded westward and developed a route for diplomatic missions and trade, later called the Silk Road. During this dynasty, paper was invented.

❖Han Xing Becomes Commander-in-Chief

韩信拜将

Han Xin was a famous general who helped defeat the Qin and establish a new empire called the Han dynasty (207 BC-AD 220). However, when Han Xin was young, he was thought to have no potential at all.

Born into a poor family in eastern China, Han Xin led an undistinguished childhood. When he became an adult, he was not recommended for a government post nor was he able to make a living through a trade. In order to survive, he sponged off others for food and shelter. Because he was useless, Han Xin was disliked around town.

One day, Han Xin tried fishing by a river outside of town. An old washerwoman, noticing how famished he looked, took him in and fed him for weeks.

"I promise to repay you someday," Han Xin said gratefully.

"Aren't you ashamed to be a man who can't even feed himself?" the woman replied. "I feed you out of pity, not with the hope of repayment."

Another time, a young butcher, the local bully, taunted Han Xin. "You look so tall and strong, and you carry your sword around, but in fact you're good-for-nothing. Go ahead. I dare you to stab me with your sword. If you're too cowardly, then crawl between my legs."

Han Xin looked the bully up and down. He shrugged. Then he got on his hands and knees and crawled between the man's legs. When word of this got out, Han Xin was jeered by everyone in town.

When Xiang Liang, the commander of rebel forces fighting against the Qin empire, passed through the town, Han Xin decided to join him. Han Xin never stood out among the other soldiers. After Xiang Liang's death, he became a bodyguard of the new commander, Xiang Yu. Han Xin tried to advise Xiang Yu, but his words always went unheard and unappreciated. He was never promoted to any position of importance.

After the fall of the Qin Empire, the famous commander Liu Bang became the King of Han, a small area in western China. Han Xin decided to desert Xiang Yu in favor of serving Liu Bang. While working for Liu Bang, he remained unnoticed until one day he committed a small offense. Finally, Han Xin was noticed, but for the wrong thing. For this, he was sentenced to death.

When it was his turn to be beheaded, Han Xin looked up at the officer in charge and said, "Does the King of Han have no wish to conquer the world? Why would he behead a valiant warrior?"

Impressed by his words and struck by his strong appearance, the officer paused to learn more about Han Xin. Han Xin convinced the officer that he did in fact have potential. Not only did the officer release him, but he also recommended Han Xin to Liu Bang. Liu Bang did not take the recommendation seriously and put Han Xin in charge of the officer's mess hall.

During this time, the prime minister, Xiao He, became acquainted with Han Xin. After a few conversations with him, Xiao He thought that Han Xin was an outstanding man with the potential to make great contributions if his talents were allowed to shine.

Not long after, during a march, a group of officers deserted Liu Bang. Prime Minister Xiao He heard that Han Xin was one of them and immediately set off in pursuit without first informing Liu Bang of where he was headed. Of course, when Liu Bang discovered several officers missing along with his prime minister, he was frantic. Losing Xiao He was like losing an arm.

Two days later, Xiao He returned. Liu Bang demanded to know why he had deserted him.

"I wasn't deserting you," replied Xiao He.
"I was chasing one of the deserters, Han Xin."
Sure enough, he had Han Xin with him.

Liu Bang was skeptical. "Officers have run off
before, and you have never chased after them."

"Other officers are common and easy to
replace, but Han Xin is unique," replied the prime minister.
"He has no equal. If you are satisfied with ruling this small region you
have now, then you do not need him. If you want to rule the whole empire,
Han Xin is the only man who can help you. If that is your plan, give Han Xin
an important position. Otherwise, he will leave again."

"Fine," replied Liu Bang. "I'll make
him a general."

"The rank of general will not keep
him here, I'm afraid."

"What, should I make him the
Commander-in-Chief, then?"
cried Liu Bang in shock.

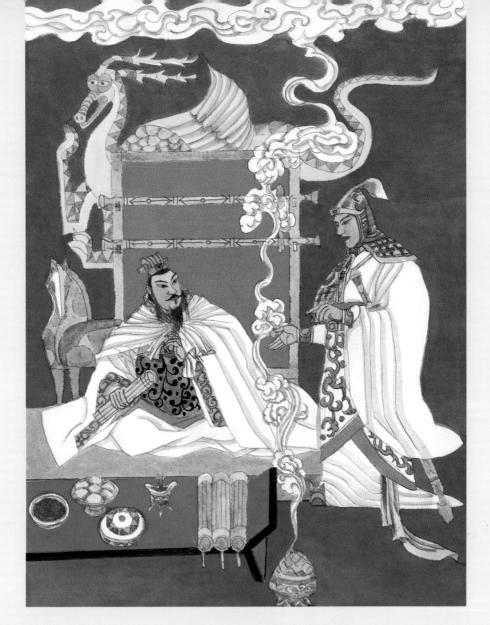

"Yes! That is a wonderful idea," Xiao He said.

Liu Bang reluctantly agreed. When Han Xin accepted the post, Liu Bang asked him, "The prime minister tells me you are an exceptional strategist. What plan do you have to help me conquer the whole empire?"

Han Xing said, "Well, is Xiang Yu your principal rival for the empire?"

Liu Bang nodded.

"Can you compete with Xiang Yu in strength and courage?" asked Han Xin.

After some thought, Liu Ban replied, "No, I cannot beat Xiang Yu."

Han Xin bowed and said, "I agree, but having served under him, I know what Xiang Yu is like. It is true that he inspires awe. When he bellows with rage, a thousand men become rooted to the ground. However, he does not trust easily and does not appoint worthy commanders. So, all of his courage is his alone.

"On the other hand, Xiang Yu is also known to be kind and generous. He sheds tears for a sick man and will offer up his own dinner to the hungry. But, if one of his men deserves a promotion, he is unwilling to share his power. His kindness is shallow, and does not make men loyal.

"Though Xiang Yu is currently the ruler of the empire, he does not have his army stationed in Guanzhong, making his control over the Central Plains questionable. He put his favorites on thrones as kings, alienating all the hereditary princes. Moreover, he has ransacked every city he passed through, making the common people detest him. Powerful as he seems now, his reign will soon decline as he loses the hearts of the people.

"You, sir, could act in the opposite way," continued Han Xin. "Rely on your bravest men without hesitation; reward those who serve you well with generosity; treat all your conquered lands with respect. Then, all the men in the empire will be more than eager to serve you.

"Now, my great king, if you issue a proclamation and lead your forces east, the whole empire will be yours!"

Liu Bang liked Han Xin's advice. He wished he had consulted with him earlier. Acting on Han Xin's recommendation, Liu Bang led his men east and conquered the central area of Qin, advanced past the Hangu Pass, and took the territory of Wei. The local kings surrendered one by one as Liu Bang and his troops marched forward.

Finally, they fought their last battle against Xiang Yu at a city called Gaixia. Han Xin and Liu Bang, with their troops, defeated Xiang Yu's army. Xiang Yu was disgraced by the defeat and killed himself by the banks of the Wu River. After this victory, Liu Bang became the first Emperor of the Han dynasty, and he appointed Han Xin as the King of the Chu state.

Later, when Han Xin returned to his homeland, he found the old washerwoman who had fed him when he was hungry. He repaid her kindness with a thousand silver pieces. He then found the bullying butcher who had insulted him.

He pointed to the butcher and told his men, "When this man insulted me so long ago, it was not that I did not dare to kill him. It was that I simply found it meaningless to do so. If I had not let him bully me then, I would never have achieved all that I have accomplished. I would not be your king today."

Illustrations by Shi Huichun and Zou Pingling

Learn more

After the fall of the Qin dynasty, a struggle emerged for power, and the country once again divided into smaller factions, led by two strong leaders, Xiang Yu and Liu Bang. With Liu Bang's ultimate victory, the Han dynasty began.

❖Zhou Chu and the Three Evils

周处除"三害"

During the Western Jin dynasty (256-316),
there lived a man named Zhou Chu. His parents
died when he was very young. Zhou Chu grew up without any guidance
or discipline, and he never finished school because he hated studying. He was a
burly man with great strength and a quick temper. He got into fights often and
caused a lot of trouble. The local townspeople disliked Zhou Chu immensely.

One day, while wandering through the town, Zhou Chu noticed that
everyone seemed glum. The townspeople walked with shoulders
hunched and eyes downcast.

Puzzled, he asked an old man, "Why is everyone so depressed?
Didn't we have a good harvest this year?"

The old man tugged on his beard and replied, "How can we be happy
while the Three Evils still plague us?"

"What are the Three Evils?" Zhou Chu asked. "I have never heard of them."

The old man explained that the first evil was
a ferocious tiger with a snow-white forehead
that lurked on the mountain to the south.
It tormented the villagers and attacked their
livestock. Local hunters were unable to capture
or kill it. The second evil was the gigantic
water moccasin that lived under the long
bridge in the river. People called the deadly
snake the water dragon and it would
appear and disappear without warning,
making it impossible to use the
river for washing or fishing.

The old man lifted his wrinkled face to Zhou Chu. "The third evil," he said with a wavering voice, "is considered the worst of all. It is you, Zhou Chu."

Zhou Chu was shocked to hear this. *Do I behave so badly that my countrymen regard me as the worst evil?* he thought to himself.

The next day, armed with bow and arrows, Zhou Chu set off onto the mountain. He hiked the steep grades, searching and searching. Finally, he spotted the tiger's footprints. He hid behind a tall tree and waited patiently. When the tiger stalked into sight, Zhou Chu fit an arrow into his bow and shot at the tiger's forehead. The arrow whistled through the still air and found its mark. In one shot, Zhou Chu killed the tiger.

Zhou Chu returned to the village and asked some hunters to help him carry away the dead tiger. Everyone was delighted to be rid of one of the evils.

A few days later, Zhou Chu armed himself with a dagger and dove into the river by the long bridge. The water dragon stirred from its sleep in the depths of the river and swam up to attack the disturbance. Zhou Chu waited with his dagger aimed until the water dragon reached the perfect position, then he lunged forward and thrust his dagger at the giant snake.

The water dragon, badly wounded, swam off downstream, leaving a trail of blood in the water. Zhou Chu swam after it.

Three days and three nights passed and Zhou Chu did not return. Rumors spread that both he and the water dragon had died in the fight, neither gaining victory. Some of the villagers felt badly about Zhou Chu's death, thinking he had given his life for their benefit. Others who had been bullied by him in the past rejoiced, cheering the end of all three evils.

During the celebration some days later, Zhou Chu returned to the village with no signs of injury. He had followed the water dragon for dozens of kilometers. He'd waited until the great snake had weakened from its wound and then Zhou Chu went in for the final kill. When he realized the celebration in progress was for his believed demise, he understood how much he was hated. Zhou Chu packed his belongings and left the village.

Zhou Chu traveled to the state of Wu in search of two famous masters, Li Ji and Li Yun. When he arrived at their home, Zhou Chu said to them, "I have made many mistakes in my life and have not been the best person. I would like to mend my ways and become a good man. Is it too late to reform?"

"It is never too late to learn, if you are determined," they answered.

From that day on, Zhou Chu studied hard under the guidance of his masters. He worked to improve his character. As he gained more and more knowledge, he turned into a man with refined moral values and upstanding behavior. He changed so much that no one who knew him before would recognize him.

Zhou Chu's impressive story soon reached the local magistrate, who gave him a position as a government official. From that post, Zhou Chu worked as an intelligent, talented, and virtuous man. Eventually, he became a minister for the Jin dynasty.

Several years later, a rebellion broke out in the northwest of China. Zhou Chu was sent as a peacemaking general to quell the revolt, but he was killed in battle. People mourned his death as the unfortunate loss of an honorable man.

Illustrations by Chen Yafei, Chen Qu, and Gao Nianhua

The Beloved Princess Wencheng in Tibet

文成公主进藏

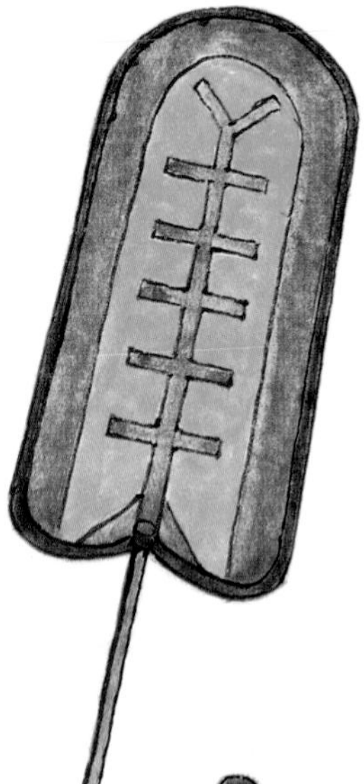

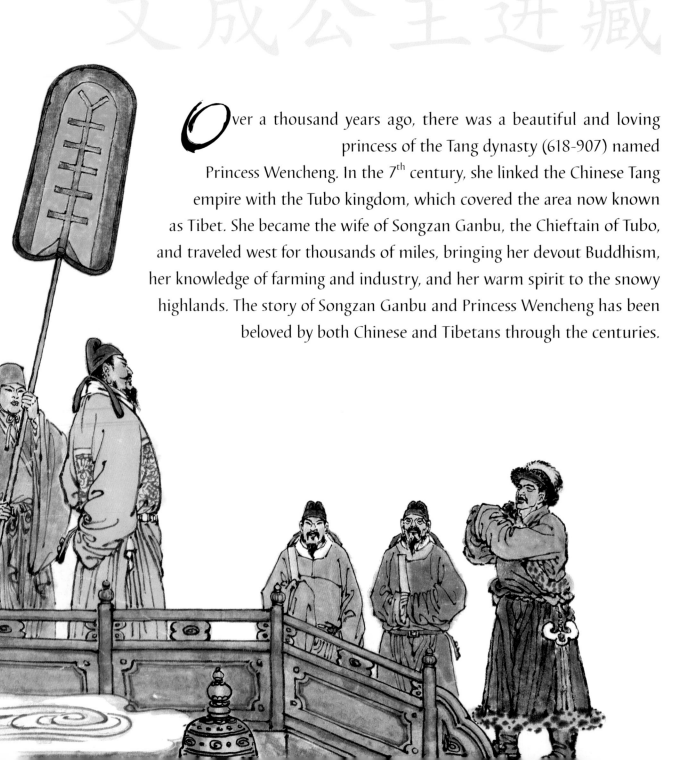

Over a thousand years ago, there was a beautiful and loving princess of the Tang dynasty (618-907) named Princess Wencheng. In the 7th century, she linked the Chinese Tang empire with the Tubo kingdom, which covered the area now known as Tibet. She became the wife of Songzan Ganbu, the Chieftain of Tubo, and traveled west for thousands of miles, bringing her devout Buddhism, her knowledge of farming and industry, and her warm spirit to the snowy highlands. The story of Songzan Ganbu and Princess Wencheng has been beloved by both Chinese and Tibetans through the centuries.

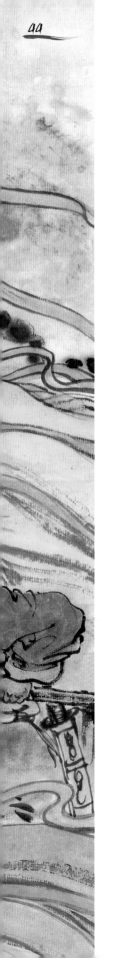

Part 1: The Four Puzzles

In 618, after years of warfare, the Tang dynasty was established with Chang-an (now Xian) as its capital. The empire had unprecedented power and wealth, and it fostered friendships with all the neighboring countries and tribes. Merchandise, money, and goodwill flowed freely in and out of the empire.

Songzan Ganbu, the Chieftain of Tubo, was a man of literary merit and military skill. He was well loved by his people. By the age of thirteen he was already an expert at riding, archery, and fencing. He was also a musician and poet. Not only was Songzan Ganbu brave and resourceful, but he was also a man of vision and ambition. One of his first acts as chieftain was to send envoys on the long and arduous journey to Chang-an to establish friendly relations with the Tang empire.

Emperor Taizong of Tang knew the good reputation of Tubo and welcomed Songzan Ganbu's envoys. He even sent envoys to pay a return visit to Tubo soon afterwards.

Pleased with the developing friendship between the two countries, Songzan Ganbu, in 641, decided to ask for a marriage with the Emperor's daughter, Princess Wencheng. He sent Lu Dongzan, his most clever and talented minister, to Chang-an with a team of one hundred men, five thousand taels of gold, and a wagon of treasures.

Lu Dongzan arrived in Chang-an and asked Emperor Taizon for the princess's hand in marriage to Songzan Ganbu. The emperor informed him that several neighboring countries had also sent envoys hoping for the princess to be married into their nations.

Emperor Taizon decided to settle the
problem by holding a contest of wits. Whoever could solve four
puzzles that he designed could marry Princess Wencheng.

For the first puzzle, Lu Dongzan was led into a garden where ten wooden
rods were lined up. Lu Dongzan had to determine which end of each
rod was the root end and which was the top. They all looked the
same on both ends. He thought for a moment, then threw the
rods into a nearby cauldron of rainwater. The root ends,
which were denser, sank lower in the water, making it
easy for him to identify which end was which.

For the second puzzle, Lu Dongzan was given a thread and a small block of jade. The jade block had a long, crooked tunnel that zigzagged nine times through the middle. The challenge was to pass the thread all the way through the crooked hole. Other competitors squinted at the hole and tried to force the thread, unsuccessfully, through the center. Lu Dongzan employed a more creative solution. He dabbed a little honey on the far end of the little tunnel. Then, he tied the thread to an ant and placed it at the opposite end of the jade block. Lured by the smell of honey, the ant crawled through the opening. Step by step the ant dragged the thread completely through the tunnel.

Lu Dongzan was then taken to a paddock full of horses for the third puzzle. One hundred mares and one hundred colts all mingled together inside the fence. Lu Dongzan had to match each mare with her own baby. While others challengers had tried incorrectly to match them by color or appearance, Lu Dongzan was the only man who matched every single pair correctly. He separated the mares and the colts for an entire night. In the morning, he released each mare one by one. The colts, missing their mothers and hungry for milk, each rushed forward to greet its own mother as she was released. In this way, Lu Dongzan paired each colt correctly with its mother.

Lu Dongzan was the only suitor to complete the first three puzzles successfully. Emperor Taizong gave him the final puzzle to try to win the Princess's hand for Songzan Ganbu. He took Lu Dongzan to a courtyard where five hundred young maidens wearing veils waited. Lu Dongzan had to identify which one was Princess Wencheng.

Lu Dongzan did not know what she looked like. He did know, however, from what he had heard about her, that she loved to wear a perfume that smelled of flowers. Looking carefully, he saw that one maiden had several bees buzzing around her head. Thus, Lu Dongzan completed all four puzzles.

Emperor Taizong was very pleased. He concluded that with such an intelligent minister, Songzan Ganbu was sure to be a man of great wisdom himself. He happily betrothed the Princess to Songzan Ganbu, ensuring an alliance between Tang and the Kingdom of Tubo.

Songzan Ganbu was delighted to hear this news. He traveled all the way from his capital in Lhasa to the edge of the kingdom to meet Princess Wencheng. There, in a town that is now in the Qinghai province of China, they were married on the shores of the Zhaling and Eling Lakes, near the source of the Yellow River. The wedding ceremony was a grand and welcoming affair.

Learn more

Tibet is located in the southwest of China on the Tibetan Plateau, the world's highest region. This is where Mount Everest, the world's highest mountain at 29,035 feet, is located.

Part 2: Princess Wencheng in Tibet

After the grand wedding ceremony of Chieftain Songzan Ganbu and Princess Wencheng, the couple set off on the long and difficult journey through the cold and rugged highlands of Qinghai and Tibet to reach Lhasa, the capital of Tubo. On the way, they stopped for a month in a town called Yushu. There, the Princess taught the villagers new methods of farming and more advanced techniques for milling flour and making wine. She gave them seeds she had brought from Tang. The villagers loved the princess so much that in 710, almost seventy years after her visit, they built a temple in her name and continue to honor her even today. This temple, open to visitors, still stands in the province of Qinghai.

As the couple traveled on through the highlands, people along the route came to greet them. Villagers prepared horses, yaks, boats, and food for the noble couple's journey. When Princess Wencheng and Songzan Ganbu finally arrived safely in Lhasa, they received the warmest of welcomes from the local people. The residents jumped with joy, and sang and danced in celebration.

At that time, Buddhism, while popular in Tang, had not been introduced to Tibet yet. Princess Wencheng was a devout Buddhist, and she had brought with her all her Buddhist scriptures and statues. She wanted to share Buddhism with the people of Tibet.

Princess Wencheng first oversaw the construction of the Dazhao Monastery. When it was completed, she and Songzan Ganbu planted willow trees in front, which later became known as the Tang Willows. Beside these willows they placed a stone tablet honoring the alliance between Tang and Tubo. Inside the monastery, the statue of Sakyamuni that Princess Wencheng had brought from Chang-an was enshrined at the center of the main hall. Statues of Songzan Ganbu and the Princess were placed in the side halls. Pilgrims who visited the monastery offered gold leaf alms to the statues. So many people made these offerings that the statues looked like they were covered with golden freckles.

Later, the princess had the Xiaozhao Temple built. She also named the mountains surrounding Lhasa after Buddhist symbols, and these names are still used today. Because of Princess Wencheng, Buddhism began to thrive in Tibet.

In addition to her work promoting Buddhism, Princess Wencheng taught the people of Lhasa new methods for growing crops. She brought corn, potatoes, soybeans, and other vegetables to the highlands. She also brought her carriages, horses, donkeys, and camels, and shared her knowledge of medicine, farming, and industrial techniques. She was a great contributor to the social and economic development of Tibet.

Meanwhile, Songzan Ganbu loved Princess Wencheng so much that he built the Potala Palace for her. Consisting of one thousand chambers, the palace was a spectacular vision of grandeur and wealth. Over the next thousand years, the Potala palace underwent many renovations and two expansions. The Potala Palace is now even more magnificent. Its thirteen stories rise 117 meters in height, covering an area of 360,000 square meters.

The marriage of Princess Wencheng and Songzan Ganbu left a long legacy of peace. For more than two hundred years following their marriage, China and Tubo maintained such a friendly relationship that hardly any fighting occurred. Envoys and merchants from both countries met frequently. People in Tibet wore Chinese silks and Tibetan children studied in Chang-an. The Tang empire sent artisans and craftsmen to Tubo to share their skills.

Songzan Ganbu is remembered today for his great leadership and vision, while Princess Wencheng is still loved for her dedication to the people of Tibet. To this day, statues of Songzan Ganbu and Princess Wencheng are worshipped in the Dazhao Monastery and in the Potala Palace in Lhasa.

Illustrations by Sheng Yuanfu

Learn more

Buddhism originated in India. Followers of Buddhism believe that one is reborn after death and the only way to break that cycle is to reach a state of nirvana by living a life of moderation and giving up personal desires. There are many different forms of Buddhism.

Buddhist temple architecture evolved over time as it spread from India. The Chinese adapted temples to their liking with a walled courtyard and several halls, each with a specific purpose, such as the depository where Buddhist scriptures and books were kept. The Xiaozhao Temple in Tibet has Chinese architectural influence because Princess Wencheng oversaw its construction.

✽Yue Fei, the Ever-Victorious General

The Song dynasty's (960-1275) most famous general, Yue Fei, was born on a cold and windy day in a farmhouse in northern China. On that day, his father paced the house, trying to think of the perfect name for his new son. Suddenly, a huge bird flew over the house with a loud screech.

"I got it!" the father shouted. He named the baby Fei, which means "to fly," in hopes that he would someday fly far and high.

When Yue Fei was only 28 days old, his father went into town. While he was there, the Yellow River flooded without warning, sending torrents of water over the land, swallowing one village after another. As the water rose, Yue Fei's mother grabbed him and jumped into a large, empty clay jar used to store water. Mother and son floated in the jar for days. When the flood finally receded, they discovered they had drifted to a small village. They decided to stay.

Yue Fei and his mother were very poor and worked in the fields for their living. Yue Fei grew up to be strong, and loved to read and learn. He was taught to be polite and respectful.

One day, an old man named Zhou Tong arrived in the village. He was a kind gentleman who was good with children and skilled in the martial arts. He began teaching Yue Fei and the other village children some basics.

Yue Fei worked hard and learned quickly. Zhou Tong began with very basic exercises such as squats and walking with bowls balanced on their heads. Little Yue Fei was impatient to do more. He complained to his mother that they weren't learning archery.

His mother said to him, "Learning martial arts is like building a house. You have to place the bricks one at a time, solidly. Otherwise, the house won't stand. The basics make you ready to learn more advanced skills."

Zhou Tong knew that Yue Fei was impatient. One day Zhou Tong took out his long bow and said to Yue Fei, "I'll make you a deal. If you can pull open this bow, I will teach you archery."

Eagerly, young Yue Fei grabbed the bow. He pulled and pulled with all his strength, but the bow's string did not budge. From that day on, Yue Fei was determined to work even harder at the basics. Eventually, he grew strong enough to pull the bow string and Zhou Tong kept his promise.

As Yue Fei grew, he became tall and strong. With his training, he became an expert in the martial arts. Not only could he pull a bow easily, but he could shoot with sharp accuracy. One day when Yue Fei was practicing archery, a rabbit hopped out of the forest before him. The rabbit stopped to munch on the grass, and it watched Yue Fei with curious eyes. Yue Fei pulled his bow, opening it fully, and aimed at the rabbit.

Suddenly, he heard a yell from behind him. "Don't shoot! Don't shoot!"

He turned around and found Zhou Tong hurrying toward him. "Martial arts are not to be used to harm the innocent," he said. "They should only be used to defend our country."

Several years later, after Yue Fei reached adulthood, he got his chance to use his skills. A group of tribes from the north called the Jin began to attack villages in northern China. They heartlessly robbed and killed villagers, and burned everything they came across. The Chinese government of the Song dynasty was weak, and the emperor ignored the people's suffering. Yue Fei was angry and worried for his countrymen. He decided to join the army and defend his country.

Although he was brave and well-trained, Yue Fei was only a foot soldier in the army. He dreamed of being a general someday. The other soldiers laughed at his dreams, but he vowed that he would someday prove himself.

One day, Yue Fei and a small troop of Song soldiers were out on patrol when they were attacked by a large company of Jin soldiers. The Jin soldiers surrounded them tightly, forcing them to fight at close range. The Song soldiers were badly outnumbered and many were killed. Enraged, Yue Fei jumped on a horse with spear in hand and headed straight for the Jin general, who was taken by surprise. The general swung his mace, but Yue Fei thrust out his spear and knocked away the mace. The general turned his horse to flee. Yue Fei chased the general and knocked him off his horse. The Jin soldiers, seeing their general fall, fled in fear.

For his bravery in battle, Yue Fei was promoted to an officer.

Over the next few years, Yue Fei led men to numerous victories against the Jin. The more he showed his talent and leadership skills, the more promotions he received. Before long, Yue Fei reached his goal of being a general. Later, he was made a Commander-in-Chief of the Song forces.

Despite Yue Fei's victories, Song still lost its vast territory in the Central Plains to the Jin. Later, the Jin took the capital of the Song dynasty and captured the emperor. Those remaining in the government fled southward and established the new capital at what is now Hangzhou. New Emperor Gao Zhong took the throne.

In the third year of Emperor Gao Zhong's reign, a famous Jin general named Wuzhu invaded Southern Song. Wuzhu was a shrewd and merciless general who was known for his invention, the *Tieguai* Armored Horses. These were armored horses that were chained together in groups of three. The three horses and their armored riders moved as one massive unit, making them hugely powerful. They won numerous battles against the Song army.

Yue Fei puzzled for a long time over how to defeat the *Tieguai* Armored Horses. Finally, he devised a brilliant, but simple, idea. He had his soldiers tie knives onto the ends of long bamboo poles.

He said to them, "All you have to do is aim the ends of the poles at the horses' legs. That is the only vulnerable area on the horse. Once one horse is hurt, all three will go down because they are chained together."

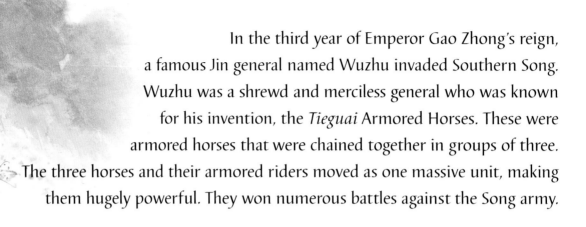

In this way, Yue Fei triumphed over Wuzhu and forced the Jin army to retreat northward. Yue Fei's fame spread throughout the country. His own army of 10,000 men became known as "Yue's Army," and the name alone struck fear in the hearts of Jin soldiers.

Yue Fei marched northward with his army and won back Song territories and cities. He drove the Jin all the way to the Yellow River and forced them to withdraw to their capital of Dongjing on the other side. Just 45 kilometers away, Yue Fei was readying his troops to cross the river and attack Dongjing when he received the emergency order from Emperor Gao Zhong to retreat.

Emperor Gao Zhong of Song and his prime minister, Qin Hui, did not want Yue Fei to succeed. They worried that if he defeated the Jin and took their capital, the former Song emperor would be rescued and returned to power. Then, Emperor Gao Zhong and Qin Hui would lose their positions. They wanted to stop Yue Fei from advancing. They continued to send emergency retreat orders. After twelve messages, Yue Fei finally gave in and returned home in grief for his country. He knew that their best chance to defeat the Jin was gone.

In 1141, Emperor Gao Zhong and Qin Hui requested a truce from Jin. General Wuzhu agreed on one condition: that Yue Fei be killed. That year, under a fabricated charge of treason, Yue Fei was imprisoned and sentenced to death. He was only 39 years old. To this day, people in China remember Yue Fei as the Ever-Victorious General, and revere him for his loyalty to his emperor.

Illustrations by Sheng Yuanfu

✤Qi Jiguang Defends China

戚继光抗倭

Part 1: The Japanese Pirates

Qi Jiguang was a renowned general of the Ming dynasty (1368-1644). His father was a military man in charge of guarding the coastal areas, and when he died, Qi Jiguang inherited his post at the age of seventeen. Because he was hardworking and disciplined, Qi Jiguang was promoted quickly, and eventually became a general with several coastal provinces under his protection.

Qi Jiguang believed that to be victorious, an army must be composed of men of high quality and discipline. He believed that it was better to have a troop of only several thousand carefully selected and trained men than a disorderly band of tens of thousands. When he arrived at his seaside post in Zhejiang province, he reviewed the local troops. The men were lazy and full of bad habits. He dismissed them all and recruited new soldiers for his army.

Drafting more than three thousand brave farmers and hardy miners from the mountainous areas in Zhejiang, Qi Jiguang organized his new army into four levels. Each group had a different job, and when coordinated properly, all the men could use their individual strengths while the entire army stayed flexible for advancing and retreating. Through strict training and discipline, this new army became an impressive and intimidating force known as Qi's Army.

At this time, the Chinese coast was plagued by attacks from Japanese pirates. The pirates harassed villages all along the southeastern coast of China.

In 1561, Qi's Army was put to the test. Japanese pirates landed on the shore outside Taizhou, a city in Zhejiang province. As soon as Qi Jiguang received the news, he relocated his army to Taizhou. They marched all night, rushing so quickly that when they arrived, the pirates had not even attacked the city yet, thinking they had plenty of time.

Just before dawn, Qi's Army opened the city gates and a thousand men streamed out silently, striking the camp of the sleeping Japanese pirates. Qi Jiguang beat the war drums himself, encouraging his soldiers. Qi's Army caught the pirates off guard and defeated them quickly. The pirates who weren't killed fled in panic.

The following year, Japanese
pirates attacked China again, but this time they struck the
Fujian province to the south, thinking that Qi's Army was too
far away to fight them. Qi Jiguang and his army rushed all the
way to Fujian and defeated the pirates again. Qi Jiguang decided
then that rushing along the coast every time the Japanese pirates
attacked was not the most efficient strategy. He wanted to put an end to
the pirates once and for all.

After a few inquiries, Qi Jiguang learned that the pirates were
headquartered on Hengyu Island, a few dozen kilometers off the coast
of Fujian. The island was a good choice for a hideout, as
its physical features made it hard to attack. There, the
Japanese pirates stored their treasures and rested
between attacks.

Qi Jiguang divided his army into two
troops, and sent one to attack from the side and the
other to attack from the front. He had heard that the
beaches were full of muddy sandbars that would bog
the soldiers down, so he ordered each soldier to carry
a wooden plank. They waited for low tide, then the
soldiers placed their planks on the muddy sand to
cross the beach easily. When the pirates discovered the army approaching, it
was too late. The other troop had already landed on the other side,
and the pirates were trapped. The battle ended with the
crushing defeat of the Japanese pirates.

With this defeat, Qi's Army established its reputation up and down the Chinese coast. Japanese pirates would flee at even the rumor of its approach. The Chinese sea villages were never bothered by pirates again.

Learn more

Japanese pirates became especially troublesome along China's coasts during the 15th and 16th centuries because there was great unrest in Japan. It was very hard to make a living in Japan so some men turned to piracy. The Japanese pirates caused trouble and violence along the Chinese coast for over 100 years.

Part 2: Fooling Fox Dong

After Qi Jiguang's success with the Japanese pirates, he was relocated to
northern China, where he was put in charge of guarding the border
from attacks from Mongolian tribes. When he arrived, he improved the
existing military operations by retraining the soldiers, upgrading
the equipment, and reinforcing sections of the Great Wall.

Once, Qi Jiguang captured a chieftain of a Mongolian tribe, who was attempting to lead his army into China at Qinshan Pass.

The chieftain's name was Fox Dong. With his army defeated, Fox Dong pleaded for his life. In order to keep good relations with the Mongolian tribes, Qi Jiguang released him.

Fox Dong, however, felt humiliated by the defeat and vowed to seek revenge against Qi Jiguang at the earliest opportunity. A few years later, Fox Dong heard that Qi Jiguang was bedridden with illness and had fewer than 2,000 soldiers defending his city of Santunying. This was Fox Dong's chance. Taking 5,000 men, he headed for Santunying, burning, killing, and looting all the way.

Qi Jiguang was indeed very ill. Hearing the news of Fox Dong's approach, he knew that if it came down to a battle, his army might be defeated. He quickly came up with a plan. He had his assistants help him dress in full armor and walk to the top of the gate tower. There he sat under the flag bearing the word Qi and awaited the arrival of Fox Dong.

Soon, the Mongolian cavalry surged in from the mountain passes. They lined up outside the gate, and Fox Dong came forward.

"Fox Dong," Qi Jiguang called from atop the tower. "Do you remember our battle at Qinshan Pass several years ago?"

Fox Dong was shocked to see Qi Jiguang. He wondered how he could be atop the tower in full armor if he was ill. He also remembered how badly his forces were beaten at Qinshan Pass.

He gathered his courage and called back, "Qi Jiguang, today I come to avenge that insult. I will wash Santunying with the blood of you and your men!"

Qi Jiguang laughed. "I have already forgiven you once. If you return now to provoke me again, you are asking only for your own death."

The more Qi Jiguang spoke, the more Fox Dong feared he had perhaps received false information. "I have brought 5,000 of my elite men to take your head," he said tentatively. He wondered if he had made a terrible mistake.

Without bothering to reply, Qi Jiguang waved his hand. Immediately, banners rose above the walls. A large number of soldiers in bright armor stepped forward on the walls, aiming guns and cannons.

"Your army is very impressive," Qi Jiguang said. "But why don't you take a look at mine?"

The city gate to the side opened and a column of soldiers marched out in procession, heading toward a training field next to the city. At the end of the procession, which took quite a while, Fox Dong figured he had seen roughly 30,000 men. He realized that if Qi Jiguang ordered his army to attack at that moment, he and his men would be chopped into meat stuffing. He immediately ordered a quick retreat, leaving behind all their supplies.

As soon as the enemy fled, Qi Jiguang collapsed with weakness. He was carried back to his bedchamber, secure in the knowledge that he had saved the city even though he truly had fewer than 2,000 men defending the walls. Where had 30,000 men come from, then?

The secret was that there was an underground tunnel linking the city and the training field. The soldiers marched out of the city gates, to the field, and then returned unseen to the city through the tunnel. They then marched out again, following tightly at the end of the line. Circling this way, they made it look like they had a large number of soldiers. And the army atop the walls with weapons? They were ordinary citizens in disguise!

Qi Jiguang recovered from his illness and eventually retired to his hometown in 1583. He died in 1588. During his military career of over forty years, Qi Jiguang spent most of his days on horseback, either fighting Japanese pirates on the southeastern coast or training soldiers in the north. He is remembered as the most famous and most patriotic general of his time.

Learn more

Mongolia is located north of China. Prior to the Ming dynasty, the Mongols invaded and conquered China, ushering in the Yuan dynasty (1279-1368). This was the first dynasty run by foreigners. The Yuan dynasty ended after a peasant rebellion defeated the Mongols and the Chinese returned to control.

The Great Wall is over 4,000 miles long and served as a protective barrier from enemies. Originally a series of separate walls erected during the Warring States period, the Great Wall became one long structure under the rule of the first emperor of the Qin dynasty. Rulers of subsequent dynasties reinforced the wall, adding improvements such as watchtowers.

❖Zheng Chenggong and the Battle for Taiwan

郑成功收复台湾

Zheng Chenggong was considered a great general and hero at the end of the Ming dynasty (1368-1644) and the beginning of the Qing dynasty (1644-1912). The Ming dynasty was led by people of the Han ancestry while the Qing dynasty was led by the Manchurians. They were thought to be barbarians from the northeast corner of China. After the Manchurian troops entered the Central Plains to defeat the Ming and established the Qing dynasty, many of the Ming dynasty's former generals still loyal to the Ming refused to surrender. They continued to fight to the very end. Zheng Chenggong was one of the brave generals who led the battle.

Zheng Chenggong's father was originally a general of the Ming, but he surrendered when Qing's army advanced to Fujian, a southeastern province on the coast. Zheng Chenggong, however, refused to surrender and fled to a small island called Nan-ao, where he enlisted several thousand men to fight against the Qing. Later, he established a navy in Xiamen, a harbor on the southeast shore.

At that time, most of Fujian was occupied by the Qing already. Zheng Chenggong's survival from one day to the next could not be ensured, yet he still had ambitions of defeating all of the Qing someday. He decided that occupying the island of Taiwan, off the southeastern coast of China, was the best tactic for developing a strategic base and strengthening his troops.

The history of Taiwan can be traced back as early
as the Han dynasty in 206 BC, when it became a territory of
China. During the Ming dynasty, it was a part of the Fujian province
and the name Taiwan came into use. Other than natives from
the original island tribes, most people in Taiwan are of Han
ancestry, immigrants from the mainland of China.

In 1642, a Dutch commander led thirteen
warships to invade the island of Taiwan. The Dutch
landed on the southwest shores of Taiwan and
established two walled cities, now known as
Tainan and Anping.

The Dutch ruled these two cities with
military law and the Taiwanese people were treated
terribly. Not only did the Dutch treat the local people as
second-class citizens, but they seized their money and property whenever
they pleased, and even forced some of the locals into slavery.

For almost twenty years, the people of Taiwan lived under these unbearable conditions. They attempted a revolt in 1652, but it failed and ended in the massacre of the rebels. This further fueled the Taiwanese hatred of the Dutch colonists.

Zheng Chenggong realized that Taiwan would be the perfect stronghold from which he could strengthen his forces and launch a counterattack, but he would first need to remove the Dutch. He mobilized his entire army for the cause, repairing warships, increasing munitions and supplies, and spying on the Dutch. His army was ready to sail across the channel and fight at his command.

In March, Zheng Chenggong had a window of opportunity. The Dutch had very few soldiers on the island at that time. Additionally, the monsoon season would make it difficult for the Dutch to send reinforcements. Zheng Chenggong and 25,000 men set sail on several hundred warships. They landed at a harbor north of Anping, where the Dutch army had very few defenses. Zheng Chenggong's troops easily defeated the soldiers there.

When people heard that
Zheng Chenggong had come to
liberate Taiwan, they rushed to
the harbor in crowds, pushing
handcarts of food and offering
the soldiers water and tea.

Zheng Chenggong, escorted
by several generals, went to visit a
local tribe called the Gaoshan to establish relations. From
the welcoming crowd, four men walked out, each bearing a plate.
On one plate was a pile of gold, and on the second, a pile of silver.
The third held a clump of weeds, and the fourth a mound of earth.
The men presented the plates to Zheng Chenggong.

With a smile, General Zheng said, "Countrymen, we have come to Taiwan with the sole purpose of driving out these cruel thugs to regain your land, not to demand gold and silver." He accepted the plates of weeds and earth, but refused the other two.

The tribal chiefs were very pleased with Zheng Chenggong's response. Prior to Zheng Chenggong's arrival, Dutch missionaries warned of the Chinese invasion. They said that General Zheng murdered people and set fire to villages in order to steal gold and silver.

The four plates they presented were a test for Zheng Chenggong, who passed, winning their trust. Word of the general's integrity soon spread all over the island, and the leaders of all the tribes expressed their wish to contribute to the cause.

By this time, General Zheng's army had forced the Dutch back into their two walled cities of Tainan and Anping. The Dutch knew they did not have a chance of winning a prolonged battle. They sent a man with a message to General Zheng to request a truce. They offered the Chinese forces ten thousand taels of silver if Zheng agreed to leave Taiwan.

Raising his eyebrows, Zheng Chenggong replied, "Taiwan was a part of China from the beginning, and we shall recover it. If you choose to remain here, we have no choice but to drive you out."

Zheng Chenggong laid siege on the two cities. Meanwhile, the Dutch sent twelve more warships to attack the Chinese by sea, but after a fierce fight of only an hour, two of the Dutch ships were destroyed and five were captured.

With no more hope of help, the Dutch occupying Taiwan finally surrendered. After 38 years, the Dutch colonists returned to their homeland.

Two generations later, Zheng Chenggong's grandson ended up surrendering to the Qing dynasty in 1683. In 1684 Taiwan officially became a province of Qing Dynasty. Although Zheng Chenggong's original intent of restoring the Ming dynasty had failed, he is still remembered as a national hero today for defeating the Dutch and driving them out of Taiwan, restoring Taiwan from a Dutch colony to a part of China.

Learn more

During the Ming dynasty, the Chinese had the best ships in the world. In fact, many of the things that made the ships and navigating the sea successful were Chinese inventions. The compass was first invented during the Warring States period and improved on during the Song dynasty (960 – 1279). The Chinese also invented movable sails and the rudder.

In 1949, when Mao Zedong took control of mainland China, many people followed the opposition leader, Chiang Kai Shek, to Taiwan, where they set up a government. Leaders in both Taiwan and China each declared themselves to be the official government of China. Though they now have two separate governments, Taiwan leans toward a pro-independence stance while mainland China maintains that Taiwan is a part of China. Despite this and China's 2005 Anti-Cessation Law that states that China may take action against Taiwan if Taiwan openly declares its independence, both sides now engage in trade and travel with one another.

*Lin Zexu, National Hero

民族英雄林则徐

Part 1: The Opium War

Lin Zexu was a government official of the Qing dynasty (1644-1912) famous for his dedication and loyalty to his country. He was born in 1785 and was an exceptionally smart child. By the time he was four years old, he could recite classic poetry and answer questions in verse.

Once, Lin Zexu's father, a schoolteacher, taught him to recite the poem, "Big Rats." He asked his father, "Why is the poem about rats?"

"The peasants work hard, yet sometimes corrupt and evil officials take whatever they want from them," his father answered. "These officials are just like big rats who don't work for their own food."

Little Lin Zexu nodded in understanding. "When I grow up, I want to punish those big rats!" he said.

When Lin Zexu grew up, he passed his civil service exams one by one, and eventually passed the national level exam to become an officer of the imperial court. He did much to improve the lives of common people. He worked hard and was promoted many times.

In 1821, during the reign of the feeble Emperor Daoguang of Qing, British merchants began selling opium to China. Opium is an extremely addictive drug. Once they started smoking it, many Chinese people were unable to stop. They became thin, sickly, weak, and idle. British merchants and the Chinese officials taking bribes became rich off of the opium trade in China. Even though it was destroying the Chinese people and their own economy, the corrupt officials selfishly did nothing to stop it. The center of the opium trade was in Guangzhou, where a port was open to British naval traders.

Lin Zexu saw what was happening and wrote a statement to Emperor
Daoguang predicting that if the opium trade was not stopped, there would
be no more able men to defend the country, and moreover, no
more silver left to support the military. Alarmed, the emperor
hurriedly appointed Lin Zexu as an imperial commissioner
and sent him to Guangzhou to enforce a ban on
opium smoking and trading.

The first thing Lin Zexu did upon his
arrival in Guangzhou was find out which
of the officials there were taking bribes.
He learned the names of twenty of them.
He then called an emergency meeting of all military and
government officials.

Lin Zexu stood before them and announced, "Some of you are
participating in the opium trade. I know who you are. Step forward and admit
your guilt yourselves, or you will suffer more serious punishment."

No one stepped forward. The corrupt officials did not believe that Lin Zexu really knew anything.

"What? No one?" Lin Zexu asked. "Very well, then." He called out all twenty names, and these officials were immediately fired and thrown in jail.

With the Chinese government in Guangzhou free of corruption, Lin Zexu turned to the British merchants. He sent soldiers to their mansions to demand all their opium. The British, however, did not believe Lin Zexu to be very strong, so they refused. Lin Zexu responded by surrounding the British neighborhood with his men and cutting off all supplies of food and water to the mansions.

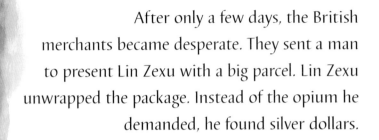

After only a few days, the British merchants became desperate. They sent a man to present Lin Zexu with a big parcel. Lin Zexu unwrapped the package. Instead of the opium he demanded, he found silver dollars.

"You are wrong to think that I can be bribed," he said. "Go back and tell your men that my patience is running out."

The British had no choice, then, but to hand over all their opium. Lin Zexu destroyed more than one billion kilograms of opium in twenty days. After that, the relationship between the British and the Chinese became tense.

Dealing with the British merchants made Lin Zexu realize that China could no longer be closed to the outside world. He decided that the Chinese should learn about politics, economics, and the culture of foreign countries in order to be prepared to interact with them. He also purchased foreign artillery, reinforced coastal defenses, and readied his troops for possible war.

In 1839, a British sailor killed a Chinese villager. Lin Zexu demanded that the murderer be punished under Chinese law and that the British sign an agreement to stop importing opium. The British refused and fighting broke out. This was the beginning of the Opium War.

With the preparations he'd made, Lin Zexu won several battles. However, the British, with their strong fleet and advanced weapons, avoided a direct confrontation with Lin Zexu and moved northward. The British captured Dinghai in the Zhejiang province, and then attacked Dagu, a port near Tianjin city, about 100 kilometers from the capital city of Beijing. Emperor Daoguang, panicking, pleaded for peace. He blamed Lin Zexu for causing the trouble and dismissed him from his post, banishing him to the city of Yili in the Xinjiang province, the farthest northwestern corner of China.

Hearing that Lin Zexu was demoted, the local people became angry. Before he left, they visited him, one after another, to offer their sympathy and gifts. So many people came to see him that the streets were jammed with crowds. They knew that Lin Zexu was a man who truly worked for the good of his country and his people.

Learn more

Being a civil servant was a very prestigious job throughout Chinese history. The first emperor of the Han dynasty understood that a successful reign needed intelligent administrators, so he instituted a civil service program. One had to pass rigorous examinations, at that time, based on the teachings of Confucius. Civil servants held local posts and through hard work and recognition, could be promoted into rewarding posts serving the imperial court.

Part 2: Exile in Xinjiang

Lin Zexu's journey into exile in Yili was long and arduous. His health was failing and he suffered from pains, nosebleeds, and fevers along the entire 3,000-mile route. Luckily, his reputation had spread throughout the country and everywhere he went, local officials and citizens welcomed him with food, lodging, and supplies.

Once, when passing through the city of Xian, over thirty officials accompanied him to the outskirts of town to see him off. Another time, a local magistrate hired for Lin Zexu five carts and two sedan chairs for his journey. After four months of traveling through rain, snow, and heat, Lin Zexu and his men finally arrived in Yili. The local general called on him immediately after his arrival to welcome him and offer him the position of treasurer for the local army.

Lin Zexu's health did not improve much after his arrival. He was often weak and ill. Already dispirited by his situation, he received a worse blow when he learned that the Qing emperor had signed the Treaty of Nanjing. A symbol of national humiliation, this treaty with the British stated that British citizens would be subjected only to British law if they committed a crime. Moreover, five more ports would be open to trade, and all of them would allow opium. Even more opium entered China after this.

Depressed, Lin Zexu wrote in a letter to a friend, "My own life is unimportant to me, but knowing that Central China is being trampled upon steals my rest. Whenever I turn around and look behind me, I am unable to eat or sleep well."

Despite these setbacks in his own life and in China, Lin Zexu continued to fight for his beliefs. When he was first exiled, his family and friends pooled their money, preparing to pay the fee for a pardon to free him. He refused their help, however, saying that he had committed no crime, and that payment would be an admission of guilt. He would rather face his exile than be recorded in history as a traitor.

Even though he'd been treated badly by the government, Lin Zexu continued to work hard for the Chinese people. One of his greatest achievements while in Yili was opening a vast area of barren land to farming by building a canal and installing irrigation. He also taught the people new agricultural techniques to increase their production.

When the emperor heard about Lin Zexu's success in farming the northern areas of Xinjiang, he ordered him to do the same in the south. The emperor did not care about Lin Zexu's poor health, or that southern Xinjiang was a vast expanse of desert sand. The weather and more diverse population of people speaking different languages meant a much more difficult life for Lin Zexu.

Still, Lin Zexu followed orders and worked diligently. He spent his days walking the land, whether it was freezing cold in winter or burning hot in summer. He crossed the Gobi Desert by uncomfortable transport and lodged in thatched cottages, yurts, and caves. He checked all canals and irrigation work personally to make sure they met his high standards. He demanded his men to do the same.

Many people could not understand why Lin Zexu worked so earnestly, or how he could still be so motivated. Because Lin Zexu was deemed a guilty man, he had to make his contributions under the name of the local officials. He was deprived of even the right to write official statements. Lin Zexu would do all the work and draft all the paperwork, but they would be signed and sent to the emperor in the name of other people. He received no official credit for his hard labors.

But, Lin Zexu did not care if he did not receive recognition as long as he was working for the good of the country. In a single year, he added six hundred and ninety thousand acres of cultivated land to the Qing government and consolidated the border defense works as well.

When the imperial decree for his pardon finally came, Lin Zexu departed for the central plains. The local people were sad to see him go. He had made a real difference in their lives, and all Chinese people remember him today as a man of great virtue and loyalty to China. He is a national hero.

Learn more

People throughout China spoke different languages, thus sometimes making communication very difficult. Today in China, while Mandarin is the national language, there are many different dialects spoken, depending on the region. Cities and towns and villages may all have their own dialect, completely different from Mandarin. For example, people in Shanghai may speak Shanghainese and Mandarin.

The Gobi Desert is the largest desert in Asia, covering 500,000 square miles from southern Mongolia to northern China. While parts of it are waterless and rocky, other parts are covered by grassy plains. A yurt is a round tent made of animal skins. It is built on a frame that can be folded for easy transport.

Library of Congress Cataloging-in-Publication Data

Zhongguo lishi gushi. English
 Chinese history stories / edited by Renee Ting.
   p. cm.
 ISBN 978-1-885008-37-4 (v. 1) -- ISBN 978-1-885008-38-1 (v. 2) 1.
 China--History--Juvenile literature. I. Ting, Renee. II. Title.
 DS735.Z453213 2009
 951--dc22

                        2009027288

Special thanks to Debbi Michiko Florence for her editing
and text contributions.

Originally published in Chinese as 中国历史故事（下）
Zhejiang Juvenile and Children's Publishing House Co., Ltd., 2008
Ren Rongrong, General Editor

Shen's Books

Walnut Creek,California
Sharing a World of Stories
800-456-6660
www.shens.com

SHEN'S
BOOKS

Book design and production by Patty Arnold, *Menagerie Design and Publishing*

Printed in China